Myth-hattan

Upper Gnome Side

Grand Cyclops Station

Centaur Park

This book is for Lucy

Giant Tess
Copyright © 2019 by Dan Yaccarino
All rights reserved. Manufactured in China.
No part of this book may be used or reproduced in any manner whatsoever without
written permission except in the case of brief quotations embodied in critical
articles and reviews. For information address HarperCollins Children's Books, a
division of HarperCollins Publishers, 195 Broadway, New York, NY 10007.
www.harpercollinschildrens.com

Library of Congress Cataloging-in-Publication Data
Names: Yaccarino, Dan, author, illustrator.
Title: Giant Tess / Dan Yaccarino.
Description: First edition. | New York, NY : Harper, [2019] |
Summary: Being the only giant around, Tess wants more than anything to be like
    everyone else, but when she and Smokey, her dragon best friend, use their height
    to help save the big parade, Tess suddenly realizes that she is just the right size.
Identifiers: LCCN 2017057331 | ISBN 9780062670274 (hardcover)
Subjects: | CYAC: Giants—Fiction. | Size—Fiction. | Self-acceptance—Fiction.
Classification: LCC PZ7.Y125 Gi 2019 | DDC [E]—dc23 LC record available at
    https://lccn.loc.gov/2017057331

The artist used brush and India ink on vellum and Photoshop to create the digital
illustrations for this book.
Typography by Celeste Knudsen
18 19 20 21 22 SCP 10 9 8 7 6 5 4 3 2 1
❖
First Edition

DAN YACCARINO

GIANT TESS

HARPER
An Imprint of HarperCollinsPublishers

Once upon a time, a baby named Tess was adopted and brought home.

She began to grow . . .

and grow . . .

and grow!

First Grade, Myth-hattan Elementary

Until no one could deny it—Tess was a giant.

A very hungry little giant!

Tess knew she was big, but what
she wanted more than anything
was to be like everyone else.

But she wasn't.

On the morning of the big parade, Tess wanted to help with the preparations.

But things didn't go as planned.

"Hey, watch it!" everyone yelled.

"I'm just too big!" Tess cried.

She wanted to hide forever.

After a while,
she heard a low,
sad howl.

"Maybe I can help," she said.

It was a dragon! And he was hurt.

She touched the spot where the dragon
was hurting and pulled out a thorn.

They not only became best friends right away,
they were the same size!

Tess named him Smokey.

The parade was now in full swing. Tess and her new friend watched from inside the park. If only they could march, too.

All of a sudden, there were screams.

A huge gust of wind had blown a parade balloon up into the air, taking someone with it. The mayor!

"We've got to help!" Tess told Smokey, and the two of them flew up to rescue the mayor in ten seconds flat.

The mayor was very grateful.

He asked Tess to be in the big parade. Smokey, too, of course!

Tess never felt she was too big ever again.

In fact, she was just the right size.

Welcome to

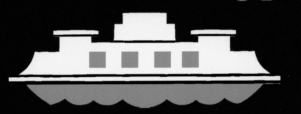

Staten Island Fairy

Hydra Street

Monster Square Garden

The Lower Beast Side